SHARKS SET I

SAND SHARKS

Heidi Mathea
ABDO Publishing Company

Published by ABDO Publishing Company, 8000 West 78th Street, Edina, Minnesota 55439. Copyright © 2011 by Abdo Consulting Group, Inc. International copyrights reserved in all countries. No part of this book may be reproduced in any form without written permission from the publisher. The Checkerboard Library™ is a trademark and logo of ABDO Publishing Company.

Printed in the United States of America, North Mankato, Minnesota.
042010
092010

 PRINTED ON RECYCLED PAPER

Cover Photo: Peter Arnold
Interior Photos: Alamy p. 17; © Andy Murch/SeaPics.com p. 8;
    Copyright © Brandon Cole p. 5; © Doug Perrine/SeaPics.com pp. 10–11;
    Getty Images p. 13; © Nigel Marsh/SeaPics.com pp. 15, 21; Photolibrary p. 19;
    Uko Gorter pp. 6–7, 9

Editor: Tamara L. Britton
Art Direction & Cover Design: Neil Klinepier

Library of Congress Cataloging-in-Publication Data

Mathea, Heidi, 1979-
  Sand sharks / Heidi Mathea.
      p. cm. -- (Sharks)
  Includes index.
  ISBN 978-1-61613-428-0
  1. Sand tiger shark--Juvenile literature. I. Title.
  QL638.95.O3M38 2011
  597.3--dc22
                          2010007271

CONTENTS

SAND SHARKS AND FAMILY

Today, there are more than 400 species of sharks. Sharks are fish covered in rough, toothlike scales called denticles. These scales provide protection for their skin.

Unlike you, sharks do not have a bony skeleton. Their skeletons are made of a tough, stretchy tissue called cartilage. Grab your ear. That's cartilage!

The sand shark is popular in public aquariums. Its large size and snaggle-tooth look attract crowds! This bulky shark is known by many different names. These include gray nurse shark, spotted ragged-tooth shark, and sand tiger shark.

The sand shark belongs to the family Odontaspididae.

What They Look Like

The sand shark has a thick body and a flattened, cone-shaped snout. There are five gill slits on either side of its head. The shark's tail, or caudal fin, is **oblong**. Its upper **lobe** is larger than the lower lobe.

Besides the tail fin, a sand shark has four other kinds of fins. Two dorsal fins, two pelvic fins, and one anal fin keep the shark stable. The shark uses its two pectoral fins to steer.

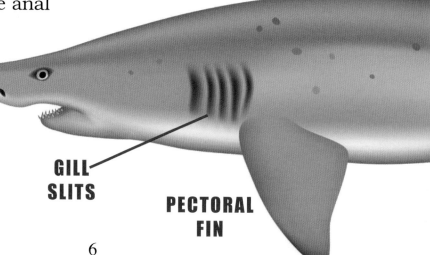

GILL SLITS

PECTORAL FIN

Pointy teeth fill the sand shark's long mouth. The teeth stick out in all directions. You can see them even when the mouth is closed!

These fierce-looking sharks are light brown or light greenish in color. They have rusty or brown spots. Their bellies are whitish.

Sand sharks are usually 4 to 9 feet (1 to 3 m) long. But, these sharks can grow bigger. The largest sand shark on record was 10.5 feet (3.2 m) long!

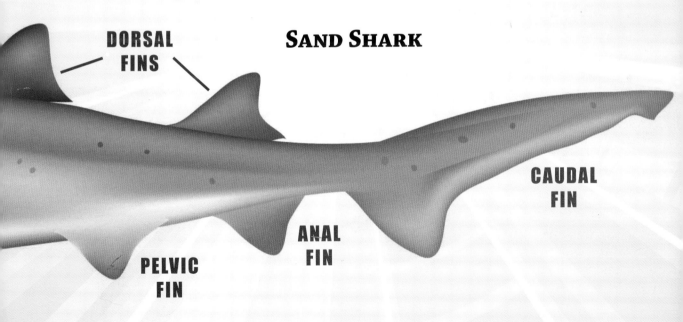

SAND SHARK

DORSAL FINS

CAUDAL FIN

ANAL FIN

PELVIC FIN

WHERE THEY LIVE

Sand sharks occupy most **temperate** and **tropical** ocean waters. However, they do not live in the eastern Pacific Ocean.

This shark received its name because it is common in shallow water near shore. But sand sharks also venture offshore. And, they can dive as far as 656 feet (200 m) below the surface.

Sand sharks prefer to remain near the ocean floor.

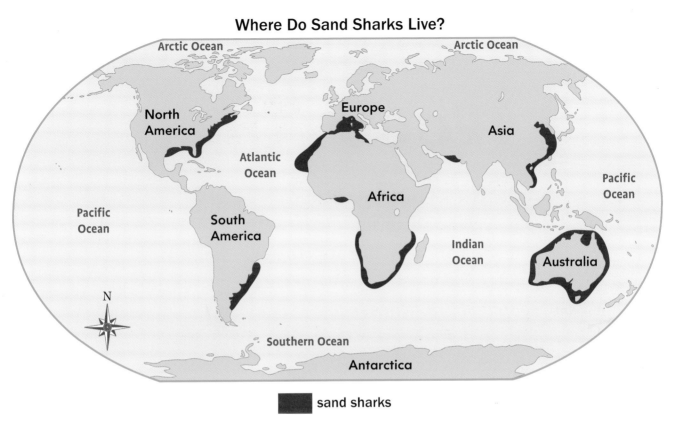

Where Do Sand Sharks Live?

sand sharks

Sand sharks are often seen along the ocean bottom. They can also be found at middle depths and at the surface.

These sharks **migrate** seasonally. In summer, they move toward the **poles** to cool off. They head for warmer water near the **equator** in fall and winter.

FOOD

Sand sharks hunt at night, staying close to the ocean floor. These large fish have big appetites! They eat a wide variety of bony fish. These include herrings, eels, bonitos, and snappers. They also feed on squids, crabs, lobsters, and smaller sharks.

Sand sharks usually swim alone. However, they have been observed hunting in schools. Together, the sharks chase prey into a tight group. Then, they feed on the trapped fish. Even with all their teeth, sand sharks swallow their prey whole.

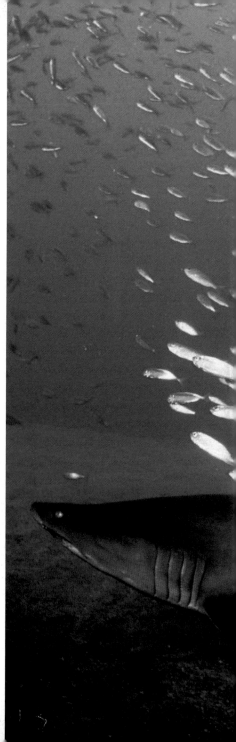

Sand sharks are fierce predators, especially when they work together!

SENSES

Visibility can be poor in seawater. To find prey in these conditions, sand sharks rely on their other senses. Sounds, vibrations, and scents travel well through water. Sharks are very sensitive to these **stimuli**.

Sharks use their ears to hear. They also use their lateral line system to detect sounds and vibrations. The lateral line consists of sense **organs** on either side of a shark's body. Sensing vibrations tells a shark about its surroundings.

Like other sharks, sand sharks can sense electric fields. For this sense, they use a system of sense organs in their heads. All living animals give off their own weak electric field. Sensing this electric field helps sand sharks navigate and find hidden prey.

Sand sharks live 15 years or more.

BABIES

Sand sharks begin life as eggs inside the mother. There, the baby sharks hatch and continue to develop.

As they grow, the babies feed on unhatched eggs. They also eat their **siblings**! Just two baby sharks, or pups, will survive this period of development.

In eight to nine months, the female shark gives birth to her young. The pups are a little more than three feet (1 m) long. They each weigh about 13 pounds (6 kg). The pups are fully developed. They can swim and eat prey right away.

After delivering her pups, the mother swims away. The newborn sharks are left on their own to try to survive.

A female sand shark gives birth once every two or three years.

ATTACK AND DEFENSE

Like other sharks, sand sharks are heavier than water. They will sink if they stop swimming. Sand sharks are the only sharks known to surface to swallow air. The sharks then hold the air in their stomachs. This allows them to float and hover motionless over the ocean floor when hunting.

Sand sharks have pointy teeth suitable for catching and piercing prey. The upper jaw holds 44 to 48 teeth. There are 41 to 46 teeth in the lower jaw.

As adults, these fierce-looking sharks have no major predators. Larger sharks prey on pups and other young sand sharks. The young sharks must use their well-developed senses to avoid capture.

When a shark attacks, its upper jaw can separate from its skull. This puts more power behind the bite, which is bad news for its victims!

ATTACKS ON HUMANS

Because of their sharp teeth and large size, sand sharks should be respected. These sluggish sharks usually attack people only when bothered first. There have been 29 reports of **unprovoked** attacks by sand sharks. Two of these were fatal.

You can still enjoy the beach without worrying about sharks. Follow a few simple rules. Avoid wearing shiny jewelry in the water. Don't swim alone, at dusk, or at night. Avoid swimming where people are fishing. Sand sharks could be nearby looking for an easy meal. They like to steal fish right off the lines!

Sand sharks look mean, but they are actually quite gentle unless bothered.

Respect sharks and the world's oceans. This will allow people and sharks to coexist harmoniously.

Sand Shark Facts

Scientific Name:

Sand shark   *Carcharias taurus*

Average Size:

Sand sharks grow 4 to 9 feet (1 to 3 m) long.

Where They're Found:

Sand sharks live along coastal areas in temperate and tropical seas.

GLOSSARY

equator - an imaginary circle around the middle of Earth. It is halfway between the North and South poles.

lobe - a rounded projecting part, as of a body part or a leaf.

migrate - to move from one place to another, often to find food.

oblong - longer than broad.

organ - a part of an animal or a plant composed of several kinds of tissues. An organ performs a specific function. The heart, liver, gallbladder, and intestines are organs of an animal.

pole - either end of Earth's axis. The North Pole and the South Pole are opposite each other.

sibling - a brother or a sister.

stimulus - something that excites the body or some part of the body to a specific activity or function.

temperate - relating to an area where average temperatures range between 50 and 55 degrees Fahrenheit (10 and 13°C).

tropical - relating to an area with an average temperature above 77 degrees Fahrenheit (25°C) where no freezing occurs.

unprovoked - not prompted to action by anything done or said.

WEB SITES

To learn more about sand sharks, visit ABDO Publishing Company on the World Wide Web at **www.abdopublishing.com**. Web sites about sand sharks are featured on our Book Links page. These links are routinely monitored and updated to provide the most current information available.

INDEX